Guinea Pig's Adventure

She searched the garden frantically. There was no sign of Timmy. Sobbing loudly, she ran back to the house to tell Mum and Steven what had happened. "The grey squirrel must have opened the cage door," she wailed. "And Timmy's gone. Maybe the squirrel's eaten him! Because he's nowhere, Mum! I've searched the whole garden."

"Squirrels don't eat guinea pigs," Mum said firmly. "Calm down, Katie love, and we'll organize a search party."

More Young Hippo Animal stories for animal lovers!

Ripper and Fang
Margaret Clarke

Hands Off Our Hens!
Jennifer Curry

Esther and the Baby Baboon
Susan Gates

Big Puss, Little Mouse
Kara May

Do you like ponies? Then you'll love Magic Pony!

PAT POSNER

Guinea Pig's Adventure

Illustrated by Anthony Lewis

To My Dad, Frank Lee

Scholastic Children's Books,
Commonwealth House, 1-19 New Oxford Street,
London WC1A 1NU, UK
a division of Scholastic Ltd
London ~ New York ~ Toronto ~ Sydney ~ Auckland

Published in the UK by Scholastic Ltd, 1998

Text copyright © Pat Posner, 1998
Illustrations copyright © Anthony Lewis, 1998

ISBN 0 590 19523 9

Typeset by Backup Creative Services, Dorset
Printed by Cox & Wyman Ltd, Reading, Berks

2 4 6 8 10 9 7 5 3 1

Chapter 1

Timmy

"Oh, Mum, thank you! It's the nicest birthday present I've ever had!" said Katie. She was down on her hands and knees, on the grass, gazing happily through the wire-netting cage door.

Gazing solemnly back at her was a white, brown and tan guinea pig.

"Smell my finger," Katie said softly,

carefully poking it through the netting, "and when you've got used to the smell of me, I'll open the door and pick you up."

The guinea pig snuffled Katie's finger then gave a small squeak.

"He's asking for a titbit," said Mum, reaching in her pocket. "Here, Katie, give him this piece of carrot."

"Has he got a name?" asked Katie. "Where did you get him from, Mum?"

"From a family a couple of streets away," replied Mum. "They're going to live abroad. I've forgotten where now, but it's somewhere hot, and guinea pigs don't like very hot weather. They called him Timmy, but you could choose another name for him."

"No. Timmy suits him," said Katie, holding the carrot so Timmy could eat it. "Besides," she added, "he must feel quite strange coming to a new home with new people. It wouldn't be fair to change his name as well."

Timmy ate the carrot quickly then squeaked again. "Is he hungry or just greedy?" Katie wondered anxiously. "No, he can't be hungry, he's still got some food in his dish. What is it, Mum? Bran and oats? Maybe he doesn't like that food, though. What else do guinea pigs eat?"

"Here's Steven," said Mum. "He's timed his arrival perfectly."

"Happy birthday, Katie," said her brother, handing her a small, flattish package.

Katie guessed what it was straight away and, after thanking Steven, quickly unwrapped her present – a book on how to look after guinea pigs.

"It says in the book they like bran and oats, fresh greens, carrots, dandelion leaves, fresh hay, clover, crusts… Perhaps that's what Timmy wants. A crust of bread."

"You'd better make it a very small crust," said Steven. "He's a fat little thing."

"He is *not!*" Katie said indignantly. "It's just the way he's standing. I'll get him out and then you'll see he isn't fat."

He *is* a bit chubby, Katie thought secretly, as she stood cuddling her new pet. But I'm not going to let Steven know I agree with him.

"See?" she said, smiling down at the small creature. "He's perfect, aren't you, Timmy?"

"I still think he's fat," said Steven. "He's got a spare tyre around his neck."

"This cage is much bigger than the one he was in," said Mum. "He'll soon run his extra fat off."

"It's a huge cage," agreed Katie. "But I wonder if I should let him—"

"No!" Guessing what Katie was going to say, Mum interrupted her firmly. "You will *not* let him run around your bedroom, Katie. Timmy stays outside. Understood?"

"Understood," Katie replied reluctantly. Then she giggled. "Just look at him, Mum! He's trying to nibble my T-shirt. Have you got any more carrot in your pocket?"

"I'll be nibbling your T-shirt in a bit," moaned Steven, holding his stomach.

"Are we getting any breakfast today, or is Fatso the only one round here who's getting fed?"

"Don't call him that," hissed Katie. "You'll hurt his feelings."

"There's a lot of them to hurt," teased Steven, tickling Timmy's head with his finger. "Still, there's no doubt about it, he's a handsome-looking fella, aren't you, boy?"

Timmy squeaked and snuffled happily. He was enjoying all this attention.

"I can't wait for Sara to see him," said Katie. "I am glad it's Saturday and there's no school. Can I phone her and tell her to come round, Mum?" Sara was Katie's best friend who lived a few doors away.

"There's no need to," said Mum. "I saw her in the supermarket with her mum last night. She said she'd come round straight after her breakfast."

"Lucky Sara, getting breakfast," said Steven meaningfully.

"Hint taken," laughed Mum. "Put Timmy back in his cage now, Katie, and we'll go and get something to eat."

"All right," agreed Katie, bending down to pop Timmy into his cage. "Oh, look!" she said, shaking her head. "He's trodden in his water dish. I'll bring him some fresh water after breakfast."

"He didn't like getting his feet wet," chuckled Steven. "Look, Katie, he's shaking the water off them."

"He's made his sawdust all wet now," Katie said, closing the cage door and securing it firmly. "I'll have to go to the pet shop and buy some sawdust and bedding and food, won't I, Mum?" she went on, as they hurried towards the house. "Will you take me later? I can use the birthday money Auntie Pamela sent me."

"There's a month's supply of everything in the garage," her mum told her. "And I'll buy everything he needs in return for you keeping your bedroom tidy and giving it a thorough clean once a week."

"Clever Mum," whispered Steven. "I bet that's the reason she got you Timmy for your birthday. To turn you into a tidy person. I'm always telling you your bedroom's like a junk shop."

"At least *my* bedroom doesn't pong of rancid socks!" Katie retorted. "I practically faint whenever I go anywhere near your room."

"You'll have to clean Timmy's cage every day or it'll smell even worse than my socks," laughed Steven. "I'll help you if you like," he added, as though he didn't mind one way or the other.

Steven likes Timmy as much as I do, Katie thought happily. And we don't even know him properly yet. "P'raps I could do it one day and you could do it the next," she suggested. "Timmy will get to know us both better then."

"You should have a birthday every day," said Steven. "It makes you almost human."

Katie pulled a face and stuck her tongue out, but she was too happy to be bothered arguing with her brother.

Chapter 2

Timmy's New Home

They'd just finished breakfast when Sara arrived. "Happy birthday, Kat," she said, handing Katie a wrapped box.

"Thank you, Scarer," replied Katie, ripping the paper off eagerly. "You *knew!*" she accused her friend, as soon as she saw Sara's present. "And you never even gave me a hint."

"Didn't know till last night when we saw your mum," said Sara. "Then I heard her telling my mum about the guinea pig. We happened to be standing by the pets' section at the time, I spotted that and asked your mum if you'd got one, she said you hadn't, so..." Sara looked anxiously at her friend. "Is it okay? I mean, I know it's for the guinea pig more than for you, but..."

"It's brill, Sara!" Katie assured her, pulling the fancy water dispenser out of its box.

"Just what Fatso needs," said Steven. "He trod in his water dish before and he didn't like getting his feet wet at all."

"Go-get lost, Steven!" Katie told her brother. "And stop calling him Fatso! His name is Timmy."

"Timmy," said Sara. "I like it. It's cool. I can't wait to see him, Kat."

"I'll wash and fill this," said Katie, taking the water dispenser to the sink, "then we'll go down and fix it in his cage."

"I'll leave you to play with your toys," teased Steven, but he winked at Sara and added, "Katie's right, it's a brill present. The chubby fella will love it." Then he laughed and dodged quickly out of the way before Katie could flick water at him.

"What a pain!" sighed Katie, when Steven had gone. "But he does like Timmy even though he calls him Fatso."

And as she filled the water dispenser, she said, "It's clever, isn't it? An upside-down bottle but the water only comes out when you suck on this bit shaped like a straw. At least," she added, "I suppose that's what happens. Hold it for me, Scarer, just here, and I'll try it out."

Sara held it in front of Katie's face, and Katie leaned forward and sucked hard on the straw.

Sara laughed as her friend choked and spluttered. "Let's hope Timmy doesn't suck as hard as you did!" she giggled, grabbing a towel to wipe Katie's face.

"Come on," said Katie, giggling herself, "let's go and see."

"Woah! He's gorgeous, Katie!" said Sara. "Are you getting him out so you can fix the water dispenser up?"

"You mean so you can hold him," guessed Katie. "Come on, Timmy," she said, opening the cage door and scooping him up, "come and meet Sara. Let him sniff your hand first, Scarer, then you can hold him."

"I thought that was dogs," said Sara, but she held her hand out and laughed as Timmy sniffed loudly at it. "You know, Kat," she went on, "I asked Mum ages ago if I could have a guinea pig. And she said…" Sara stopped talking suddenly and nibbled her lip.

"What? What did she say?" Katie demanded anxiously.

"Only that she'd read somewhere that it wasn't fair to keep just one guinea pig 'cos they get lonely. You should always have two or more."

"Well, your parents are both out at work all day," said Katie. "My mum's here all day, remember. She'll be able to come down and talk to Timmy while Steven and I are at school."

"Of course. And the little monsters will like coming to see him, too," chuckled Sara. Katie's mum was a child-minder, and "the little monsters" was the name Katie had given to the three young children she looked after.

"Yes, so Timmy won't get lonely at all, will you, Timmy-boy!"

Timmy blinked and made his funny little squeaking noise. Katie made squeaking noises back, then handed him to Sara.

"I ought to show him how to get a drink before I fix this in his cage," she said. "Look, Timmy, you have to suck like this." This time Katie sucked gently on the straw.

"He's watching you, he's really watching you!" said Sara. "Give him a go now, Kat. Hold it near his mouth and see what he does."

Timmy sniffed and snuffled for a second then sucked eagerly on the metal straw. He swallowed, squeaked and sucked again.

"So clever," praised Katie. "Say thank you to Sara, Timmy. She brought this for you. Now, I'm going to fix it in your cage."

"Timmy! That's no way to say thank you!" chuckled Sara as Katie knelt down to work out the best place for the water dispenser to go. "He's nibbling my T-shirt, Kat!"

"He did that to me earlier on," said Katie. "P'raps he wants something to gnaw at."

"You could put a small log and some branches in his cage," suggested her friend. "Shall I go and look for some with Timmy?"

"Mm, good idea," agreed Katie.

Timmy wriggled like mad when Sara picked up a small branch and held it towards him. "Katie was right," said Sara. "You *do* want something to gnaw at, don't you? We'll find a couple more things, Timmy, then you can go back in your cage with them."

Before long, Timmy was scurrying about his cage, clambering over the small log, gnawing at a branch, getting a drink of water, sniffing, squeaking and snuffling all the time. Katie and Sara laughed quietly as they watched him.

Then, after a while, he picked up a twig and scurried into his bedroom area where they couldn't see him.

"We'll leave him to have a rest," said Katie. "The excitement and the exercise have probably tired him out."

"I'd better be going anyway," said Sara. "I told Mum I'd make a salad for lunch. I'll save some lettuce leaves and carrots for Timmy and bring them round when I come for your birthday tea."

"Great," said Katie, smiling happily. She *was* enjoying her birthday.

Chapter 3

Timmy Goes Exploring

Steven and Katie took it in turns to clean Timmy's cage, as Katie had suggested. And at weekends, Sara helped, too.

Timmy liked his new home and his new owner and her brother and her friend. He liked the little children who brought him dandelion leaves every day. He liked Katie cuddling him and brushing and combing him.

Can YOU read four Young Hippo books?

The Young Hippo is sending a special prize to everyone who collects any four of these stickers, which can be found in Young Hippo books.

This is one sticker to stick on your own Young Hippo Readometer Card!

Collect four stickers and fill up your Readometer Card

There are all these stickers to collect too!

Get your Young Hippo Readometer Card from your local bookshop, or by sending your name and address to:

Young Hippo Readometer Card Requests, Scholastic Children's Books, 6th Floor, Commonwealth House, 1-19 New Oxford Street, London WC1A 1NU

Offer begins March 1997

This offer is subject to availability and is valid in the UK and the Republic of Ireland only.

But he wasn't so keen on the visitor who started arriving early every morning after a couple of weeks. It chattered noisily and poked its claw through Timmy's cage door, trying to reach Timmy's food.

"I'm Squirrel and I'm hungry," the visitor said one morning. "I've heard your owner calling you Timmy. That's a funny thing to be," he added rudely. "I've never heard of an animal called a Timmy before."

"Caw-caw-caw! Caw-caw-caw! I've never heard of a Timmy either," laughed Crow, who'd flown down to see what Squirrel was doing.

Timmy quite liked the big black bird even though it had laughed. He liked it because it had frightened Squirrel away.

And for the next few mornings, Squirrel didn't come.

Then, very early one Saturday morning, Squirrel turned up again. And extremely pleased with himself he was, too. Squirrel had learned how to open cage doors!

That meant he'd be able to open Timmy's door. He'd open it wide, while Timmy was still sleeping, and then hide. And when Timmy woke up and saw the cage door was open…

Squirrel licked his lips. He was sure Timmy would be curious enough to walk out of his cage and go exploring. Then *he*, Squirrel, would nip in and eat Timmy's food.

An hour later, when Katie went down the garden to visit Timmy, she was just in time to see Squirrel scampering out of the cage. The empty cage!

She searched the garden frantically. There was no sign of Timmy. Sobbing loudly, she ran back to the house to tell Mum and Steven what had happened. "The grey squirrel must have opened the cage door," she wailed. "And Timmy's gone. Maybe the squirrel's eaten him! Because he's nowhere, Mum! I've searched the whole garden."

"Squirrels don't eat guinea pigs," Mum said firmly. "Calm down, Katie love, and we'll organize a search party."

"I'll go round for Sara," said Steven. "Then I'll cycle to the house you got Timmy from, Mum. Maybe guinea pigs find their way back to their old homes, like cats do."

"But he's happy here, I'm sure he is," protested Katie. "Nobody could love him and look after him more than I do. Unless ..." she gulped, "... unless Sara was right. She said one guinea pig gets lonely on its own. She said you should have two or more. Maybe he was lonely, Mum. Maybe that's why he's run away!"

"I don't think he *has* run away, Katie." Her mum spoke comfortingly. "I think he's just gone exploring. And I'm sure we'll soon find him, safe and sound. He can't have gone far."

Timmy, though, had managed to get quite a long way away. Squirrel's crafty plan had worked perfectly. Timmy hadn't been able to resist stepping out of his cage when he'd seen the open door. Hadn't been able to resist taking himself off for a walk. Well, more of a run at first, in case Katie came.

Timmy hadn't really noticed where he was going. Hadn't realized that the hole in the hedge he'd wriggled through led to the big, wide world outside the garden.

Though Timmy did begin to wonder exactly *where* he was after he had seen something really frightening. His plump little body was still trembling slightly from the shock of it! The shock of seeing two tall sticks walking on their own. Two tall sticks with grey feathers on. Sticks that had not only talked but had also…

Timmy shuddered. "*No!* I won't think about *that!*" he told himself firmly. "I got away all right and ... and..." he lifted his head and peered nervously around. "And there's nothing following me. I must be safe now. Still, I'd better not slow down just yet."

He scurried on for a little way until he felt *sure* he was safe. Then he stopped to catch his breath. But the next minute...

Chapter 4

Timmy Meets Water Vole

"What are you doing in my part of the dyke?" demanded a furious voice.

"Your part? Your part? What do you mean, your part?" replied Timmy, trying not to squeak with fright. He moved to one side, taking cover in the long grass. To avoid the drops of water, he told himself, for whatever had spoken to him was shaking water from his fur.

I'm bigger than him really, thought Timmy. His legs are longer so he looks taller and he's got a hairy tail which makes him look longer than me and he's quite skinny. But we look a *little* bit alike. He's all the same colour though, a sort of reddish-brown like my cage. And... Ooh, he's moving closer!

The two faced each other warily, both half-afraid of the other. But, after snuffling the air, they sensed there was no danger and the conversation continued in a friendlier manner.

"I've just been for a swim," said the creature. "But I live in this part of the dyke. That's why I call it *my* part. See, my home is just there." He pointed to a hole in the bank where the ground sloped downwards to the water-filled ditch. "It's got two doorways," he added proudly. "That one under the water and another one that opens on to the bank."

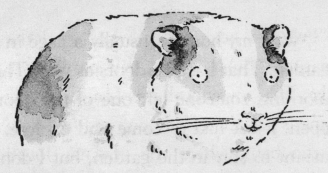

"Very nice," Timmy said politely.

"I've never seen anything quite like you before," Timmy's new friend told him. "What are you and what are you doing here?"

On a dead bough, overhanging the dyke, sat a brightly-coloured kingfisher. He thrust his head forward and waited eagerly for the answer.

"Well, *my* home is usually a cage in a garden. That has two doors as well. This morning, someone left one of the doors open. I just had to come and explore. I meant to stay in the garden, but I don't think I'm still in it, am I?"

"Indeed you are *not* in a garden!" said his companion.

"Well, perhaps you could show me around? I don't want to swim, though. I am…" Timmy thought hard. What should he say? Katie called him Timmy and that sounded friendly, but he remembered all too well how Squirrel and Crow had laughed at that and said they'd never heard of an animal called a Timmy!

"I am Guinea Pig," he stated firmly. "How do you do?"

"Oh, nicely, thank you. I'm Water Vole. Sometimes mistaken for Water Rat, I'm afraid," he added disgustedly. "But I'm altogether a much pleasanter creature."

Timmy blinked and murmured politely, "I'm sure you are."

"I suppose I could show you around," said Water Vole. "Have you seen anything at all since you came out of your garden? Apart from me, that is."

Timmy shuddered slightly as he remembered *what* he had seen. "Yes. Yes, I have seen something. It was most peculiar."

Timmy shuddered again, then he said, "I saw some grey feathers going for a walk on two tall, light-brown sticks. I was walking along the grassy path but the feathers on sticks looked so funny, I scampered down the slope to get a closer look. When I did, I couldn't stop laughing. I think laughing was a mistake though, because—"

"Did they say anything to you?" Water Vole interrupted, thoughtfully combing his wet fur with his claws.

"Yes. It must have been in stick language though because I couldn't understand it. Hang on a minute, I'll try and think of the exact words."

Water Vole was just starting to get impatient when Timmy said, "I think this is what it was!" And, holding his head up as high as possible, Timmy said slowly:

"Though my gait may seem peculiar,
regard and please observe,
my neck is all a-quiver
with extraordinary verve."

Then, Timmy lowered his head, nibbled his lip and confessed, "That's when I thought laughing had been a mistake and I ran away, back up the slope. You see, as soon as the talking stopped, this long grey thing with a yellowish bit on the end shot out from the top of the sticks. I was quite frightened. Actually, I was *very* frightened."

Water Vole groaned and moaned softly to himself. On the dead bough above them, Kingfisher chattered angrily. "Chi-kee! Chi-kee! Chi-kee!"

Chapter 5

Timmy's Grey Feathers on Tall Sticks

Timmy looked from Water Vole to Kingfisher in astonishment. What were they so upset about? Then a big green frog landed beside him, making him jump.

"Did I hear what I thought I heard?" asked Frog.

"I'm afraid so," groaned Water Vole. "Heron is around."

"Around where?" asked Timmy, peering round. Then he realized he didn't know what he was looking for. "What *is* Heron?" he asked.

"Heron is your grey feathers on two tall sticks," said Water Vole. "And he eats voles and frogs."

Kingfisher suddenly streaked like a bright blue arrow into the water, and seizing a small fish, swallowed it head first. Then he joined the others on the bank. "We'll have to do something about Heron. He has no right coming to our part of the dyke. He'll catch all the fish, leaving none for me."

Frog croaked angrily. "Maybe we should do something about you as well, Kingfisher. I've seen *you* swallowing tadpoles before now."

"Tadpoles turn into frogs," Water Vole whispered to Timmy. "That's why Frog is a bit angry with Kingfisher."

Sometimes Water Vole swallowed tadpoles and little frogs, too, but he wasn't going to admit it.

"I only eat tadpoles when I'm starving and can't find any fish," soothed Kingfisher. "And, unlike Heron, whether I feed on fish or tadpoles, I don't take them all. We must make him go away from the dyke."

"You mean so he can eat all the fish from somewhere else?" asked Timmy.

"Not exactly," said Kingfisher. "You see," he explained, "if we can make Heron go away he'll go to the main river. There are lots of fish and tadpoles there. Even Heron couldn't eat them all."

"*How* can we make him go away?" demanded Frog.

"And make him *not* want to come back," added Water Vole. "How about getting the bees to swarm round him? That would be quite frightening. They'll be in the clover patch or that hedge where the wild roses are blooming. Shall I go and fetch them?"

Timmy tried not to squeak. He didn't like bees very much. He had once accidentally trodden on a bee and he could still remember the angry buzzing noise the bee had made. He'd make sure not to move at all – not to twitch so much as a whisker – if Water Vole fetched the bees.

But to Timmy's relief, Kingfisher said he had a better idea than getting the bees to swarm round Heron.

"Let's hear this better idea then," said Frog, who still couldn't quite forgive Kingfisher for having eaten a few tadpoles.

"Find Heron and get him near my nesting hole," Kingfisher shrilled excitedly. "That's all we need to do."

"Of course, of course," agreed Water Vole and Frog.

"But why?" asked Timmy. "I thought you wanted to make him go away?"

"You'd better tell Guinea Pig about your nesting hole," Frog said to the stumpy little bird. "And while you're telling him, I'll have a think."

"Well," said Kingfisher, "Mrs Kingfisher and I took it in turns to bore a tunnel in the bank of the dyke."

"With their beaks," Water Vole said, quickly answering the question Timmy had been about to ask. "Nearly a metre long," he added, in case Timmy wanted to know that, too.

Kingfisher impatiently tapped a tiny red foot on the ground. "I thought *I* was meant to be telling Guinea Pig about my nesting hole," he said.

"Sorry, Kingfisher. Do carry on," said Water Vole.

"We made the tunnel slope upwards from the entrance hole," explained Kingfisher, "and widened it at the end to make room for the nest. Well, I suppose a bed is a better name for it than a nest.

A bed of old fish bones. You see," continued Kingfisher, looking rather ashamed, "we bring up all the bones and scales of the fish we eat. Because we swallow fish whole, we have to get rid of the bits we can't digest.

So, I'm afraid it gets rather smelly in and around our nesting hole. That's why we've got to get Heron there."

"I still don't understand," said Timmy, shaking his head.

"It's more than 'rather smelly' by Kingfisher's nesting hole," said Frog. "It's *very, very* smelly. Heron wouldn't like the smell at all. It would certainly make him go away. The problem is, how do we get him there? That's what I was having a think about."

"Ask if he'd like to be taken to a place where there's hundreds of fish, of course," said Kingfisher. "Then take him close to my nesting hole, like I said."

"Yes, yes. But which one of us could take that chance?" croaked Frog.

"I see what you mean," said Kingfisher. "*You* can't offer to take him. He would eat you. He'd eat Water Vole, too. And he wouldn't believe me if I said I'd show him where there were lots of fish. He knows I'd never do that!"

For a while they stood silent and still. Then, with one accord, Water Vole, Kingfisher and Frog turned their heads to stare at Guinea Pig.

Chapter 6

Timmy and Kingfisher

Timmy blinked and wondered why the others were looking at him so hard. Then Water Vole nodded and said, "Heron *wouldn't* eat Guinea Pig. He's too fat."

"I am not fat!" Timmy denied huffily. But then he remembered Katie's brother saying he was fat. Suddenly, he wished he was back in the place he knew and liked.

"Don't go getting upset, Guinea Pig. Water Vole didn't mean you're fat. Just that you're too fat for Heron to eat," said Kingfisher. "How about it?" he continued hopefully. "Will you do it? If I show you where my nesting hole is, then help you find Heron, will you get him there with the story about lots of fish?"

"But ... but what if he shoots that long grey thing with a yellowish bit on the end at me?" asked Timmy nervously.

Water Vole tried not to laugh and nearly choked on a bit of reed he'd been nibbling. When he'd recovered he said, "The long grey thing is Heron's neck – with his head and beak on the end, of course."

"It's nothing for you to worry about," said Kingfisher. "Heron won't be interested in eating you, he'll only be interested in the fish in the dyke."

"Then after a while the terrible smell will make him fly away," croaked Frog. "And, hopefully, he won't come back."

"You are going to do it, aren't you?" Water Vole asked Timmy. "After all, you did say you wanted to be shown around. It's just that Kingfisher will be showing you instead of me."

"Yes, yes, of course I'll do it," Timmy agreed bravely. "Come on, Kingfisher, show me the way before I change my mind."

So, Timmy and Kingfisher went off together. Kingfisher didn't stay on the ground for long. His tiny feet were good for perching on boughs but weren't very good for walking or hopping along.

Most of the time he flew just ahead of Timmy, but every so often he flew off to see if he could spot Heron.

"Slight change of plan, Guinea Pig," he chattered excitedly after one such excursion. "I've spotted Heron and he isn't very far away from my nesting hole. I'll stay with you until you can see him too. Then I'll fly ahead and tell Mrs Kingfisher what to expect. We'll have to make sure our babies stay inside. Heron has been known to eat young birdlings. When you get up to Heron talk to him for a couple of minutes then offer to show him where the fish are."

"But I won't know where to take him if I don't see your nesting hole first," protested Timmy.

"Heron being where he is has made it easy," said Kingfisher. "You'll just need to walk in a straight line. You can stop just after you pass the willow. That should be near enough to…"

Kingfisher stopped chattering as he noticed Timmy shaking his head. "I don't know what a willow is," said Timmy.

"Chi-kee!" said Kingfisher impatiently. "It's a tree."

"Is this willow the only tree?" asked Timmy. "You see I don't really know one tree from another."

"There's a hawthorn tree and an alder and... Chi-kee, there are quite a few trees before you get to the willow. All right, I've thought of another landmark. Poppies. You know what poppies look like, don't you? Red poppies, I mean.

There's a patch of them on top of the bank just above my nesting hole. You can't miss seeing them. They're so bright you can see them from a long way away. Just keep walking until they're only a little way off."

Timmy had no idea what poppies looked like either. But Kingfisher had seemed so annoyed about the trees, he just nodded his head. Besides, he knew what red looked like. His food dish was red.

"Right then," said Kingfisher. "And look, there's Heron. See, just along there, down at the edge of the water."

Timmy screwed his eyes up and peered into the distance. He was beginning to feel nervous again and half hoped he wouldn't be able to see Heron.

"Actually, I'm not sure if I can see him," he said. "I'm rather short-sighted and the sun is in my eyes."

"Well, just keep walking in a straight line, look downwards every now and then and you won't be able to miss seeing him," said Kingfisher. He was beginning to get a bit fed up with Guinea Pig. Guinea Pig didn't seem to know much about anything.

Still, he is trying to help us, Kingfisher reminded himself. So he said kindly, "Don't worry, it will work out right in the end. Find Heron first, talk to him for a minute or two, tell him about the fish, then get him to follow you until you see the poppies."

And Kingfisher flew off, leaving Timmy feeling very much alone. If I knew my way home, I'd go, thought poor Timmy. But I don't think I do. I'll just have to do what the others want me to do and hope they can show me the way home when it's all over.

Taking a deep breath, Timmy scampered along until he was sure he could see Heron. This time it looked as though the grey feathers were on one tall light-brown stick.

Heron was standing, like he often did, on one leg.

Then Timmy had a good idea. He knew how to keep Heron talking for a couple of minutes.

Chapter 7

Timmy's Brave Adventure

Timmy scuttled down the sloping bank, walked right up to Heron and said, "Good morning, I'm … I am Guinea Pig. Could you please tell me, if you don't mind, of course, why you are standing like that?"

Heron glanced scornfully down at Timmy. Then in a deep, posh voice

he said,

"*Just supposing, instead of reposing,*
I lay with my legs in the air.
Informally dozing, my claws and my toes in,
the fish passing by over there."

Once again, Timmy didn't really understand what Heron was talking about. But he couldn't stop himself from chuckling at the bit he *had* understood. He was thinking what a funny sight it would be to see those long tall sticks standing up in the air!

As the long grey neck shot out towards him, Timmy backed away and gabbled quickly, "I'm sorry, I wasn't laughing at you. I really came to tell you about a place I know. A place where there's a lot of fish. Shall I show you? Follow me."

Timmy didn't wait for an answer. He didn't think he'd be able to understand it anyway. Besides, he was scared of that long grey neck. And being scared might have made him lose weight. He might not be too fat for Heron to eat now!

That thought made him scamper back up to the top of the bank. Surely Heron would stay below, closer to the water in the dyke?

After a while, Timmy peered down, then began to chuckle again. Heron was walking slowly along the water's edge.

He had a most peculiar walk. He looked more than ever like grey feathers on top of two tall sticks. Sticks that walked in a funny way.

Timmy scampered on and soon he came to a clump of flowers. Pink flowers. They weren't poppies, were they? He had gone past two or three trees. But these were the first flowers he'd seen.

Pink flowers. Kingfisher hadn't said anything about pink flowers. Timmy felt worried. Was he going the right way?

But suddenly he found the willow. Being more short-sighted than ever because he was worried, he didn't notice the tree until his nose met the trunk with a bang!

Before he went rolling down the bank, he just had time to notice a clump of bright red flowers a little way ahead. Poppies! He *had* come the right way.

Luckily, Timmy managed to stop rolling before he reached the water. Scrambling to his feet, he peered round for Heron.

Two tall sticks sprayed Timmy with droplets of water. Heron had arrived!

"This is the place," said Timmy.

Heron curved his long neck to look down, then un-curved it and sniffed the air.

I don't know how he can bear to do that! thought Timmy. It smells *awful* round here!

Heron obviously decided he didn't like the smell either, because he stopped sniffing and looked snootily at Timmy.

Then he said,

"The stench is so appalling,
I'd find it rather galling
to have to fish just here.
Besides, my wife is calling,
she must have got a haul in,
I'll go where the air is clear."

"Grey feathers flying on two tall sticks," said Timmy, looking upwards.

And just then Kingfisher and Mrs Kingfisher popped out of their nesting hole. "Heron's going. I knew my idea would work!" Kingfisher chi-keed proudly to his wife.

Timmy blinked and gasped at the bright beauty of the two kingfisher birds.

But gasping had been a mistake. Timmy rubbed his nose on the ground, trying to get rid of the terrible smell he'd breathed in. He just couldn't understand how such pretty birds could possibly live in such a smelly place!

"I'd better go back and tell Water Vole and Frog that Heron's gone," said Timmy. He was glad of an excuse to move away from what Heron had rightly called the appalling stench!

"All right, and thank you for your help," said Kingfisher.

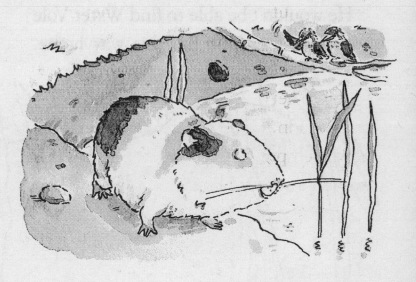

Soon, though, Timmy realized he wasn't sure which way to go. Then he remembered about his tracks!

He should sniff the ground and follow the smell of his own tracks. They'd still be fresh enough to guide him at least part of the way back to Water Vole and Frog.

But it was no good, his nose was too full of the smell of fish bones for him to smell anything else!

He wouldn't be able to find Water Vole and Frog, let alone find his way home.

And Kingfisher had gone back into the
nesting hole with Mrs Kingfisher. He was
all alone. Alone and tired and scared and
lost. Really lost!

Timmy whimpered plaintively to
himself. He was frightened of making too
much noise in case there was an unseen
something around. Something that ate
guinea pigs! After all, Heron ate frogs
and water voles, didn't he? And even
friendly Kingfisher ate fish!

Then Timmy saw something coming towards him. Four somethings! Big somethings, moving slowly ... stopping ... moving again! Close now, very close. They were going to pounce on him and eat him!

This time he whimpered loudly. Very loudly! He couldn't help it. He was terrified. He closed his eyes and tried to push his trembling body into the ground.

But the four somethings stopped right by him. He could feel them almost touching him. They'd seen him. He knew they had! Then he felt two things closing around his body and lifting him. Felt warm drops dripping on him! It must be saliva from something's mouth. He was about to get eaten!

Chapter 8

Timmy's Home Again

"Timmy, oh Timmy, we've found you at last!" Laughing and crying at the same time, Katie held him close. "Scarer, he's all right. Look, he's all right. I don't know why I'm crying!"

"Happy tears," said Sara, sniffling herself as she stroked Timmy and hugged Katie. "And, just think, Kat, we were about to turn back! I can't believe he got this far."

Feet! thought Timmy. That's what those four somethings were. Sara's feet and Katie's feet. And the two things were Katie's hands and those drops I felt were Katie's tears. Katie was crying.

Katie ... she was still stroking him. Timmy squeaked contentedly, his adventure already fading a bit from his mind.

"We'd better hurry home," said Katie,
sniffling a bit. "Mum will have a search
party out for *us* soon. We were supposed
to meet up with her and Steven ages
ago."

"Isn't that your mum?" Sara pointed
into the distance. "It is, Kat. She's come
looking for us."

The two girls waved wildly to let her know they were all right. To let her know *everything* was all right. They'd found Timmy.

"Bring Timmy indoors for a while, Katie," said her mum when they got home. "And you phone your mum, Sara, to let her know you're back. You're *all* back," she added, stroking Timmy, who was by now fast asleep in Katie's arms.

"Steven's gone to buy some little padlocks and keys and he's going to fix metal hooks and eyes on the cage doors so I can lock them," Katie told Sara when her friend came back into the kitchen after making her phone call. "Even a clever-clogs grey squirrel won't be able to undo a locked padlock!"

"I shouldn't think Timmy would want to go exploring again, anyway," said Sara. "He must have found it a bit dull and lonely just walking along the bank all on his own!"

"You're probably right," laughed Katie's mum. "But *we* don't want any more shocks and excursions like we had today."

Katie did get one more shock, though. A few days later when she went down the garden to feed Timmy, she found not one guinea pig but four. Timmy and three baby guinea pigs!

"Woah! What a surprise, Timmy," Katie said softly. "But they're beautiful, so beautiful. They look just like tiny copies of you. I didn't know baby guinea pigs were born with all their hair on!"

"Baby guinea pigs?" said Steven, coming up behind his sister. "Has Timmy had babies? No wonder he was so chubby! I bet the people who sold him knew he ... *she* was going to be a mum."

"Well, I'm glad they didn't tell *our* mum," laughed Katie. "She might not have bought a girl-soon-to-be-a-mum guinea pig!"

Katie and Steven gazed and gazed at the babies. Two were suckling milk from Timmy and one was moving round, snuffling the cage floor. It turned to face Katie and she gasped. "Its eyes are open, Steven!" she whispered. "Oh, I do wish I could pick one up and have a cuddle. They're so cute."

But Katie knew it was wrong to handle newborn animals. "We shouldn't stay here watching them much longer," she said reluctantly. "They need peace and quiet and privacy. Besides, I need to look a few things up in my guinea pig book. I expect Timmy'll need extra food and some milk to drink now there are babies to look after."

"I'll leave you to break the news to Mum," said Steven. "I'm going to the paper shop to see why my computer mag wasn't delivered this morning."

Katie ran back to the house to look in her guinea pig book and sat on the bottom stair to read it. Yes, she was right, Timmy would need extra food and some milk for a while.

And the book said baby guinea pigs were born with their eyes open, with a full coat and … Katie read the next bit aloud, "with their teeth already cut, after about sixty-five days. That's a bit over

nine weeks!" Katie worked out. "Steven was right. The people who sold him to Mum must have known he was ... I mean *she* was having babies. I'll have to call him ... I mean her..."

"Talking to yourself, Katie?" asked Mum, coming into the hall.

"Just thinking that we'll have to call Timmy *Tammy* from now on," said Katie. "Because – guess what, Mum? He's had babies!"

Mum was so shocked she had to sit down on the stairs next to Katie. She opened her mouth to speak but nothing came out.

"Don't worry, Mum," soothed Katie. "I've already thought what to do. I was wondering if, when they're ready to leave Tammy, Scarer's mum would let her have two baby guinea pigs for her birthday? I'll phone and ask her."

"Oh, Katie!" groaned Mum, as Katie got up and went over to the phone. "I didn't know I'd bought you *three* guinea pigs for your birthday!"

"You didn't," chuckled Katie as she stabbed Sara's number. "You bought *four*. I thought we'd keep one for Steven. He can call it Fatso if he likes, 'cos Timmy, I mean Tammy, won't be fat now!"

"Is that you, Kat?" came Sara's voice from the other end of the phone.

"Yes. Listen, Scarer, d'you think your mum would let me give you two guinea pigs for your birthday?"

Sara burbled loads of questions down the phone and, when she could get a word in edgeways, Katie told her friend what had happened. "And they're ready to leave their mother when they're about six or seven weeks old," she said. "That'll be just in time for your birthday, Scarer!"

Then Katie waited impatiently, pressing the phone close to her ear, while Sara went to find her mum.

"She says *yes!*" Sara shrieked, nearly deafening Katie.

"Woah! We can start a guinea pig club!" said Katie. But she was talking to herself. Sara was on her way round already to have a quick peep at her future pets.

"Look, Kat," said Sara, as the two friends hurried down the garden to Tammy's cage, "there's a heron standing at the edge of the monsters' paddling pool."

"Looking at the fish, I expect," said Katie.

"I didn't know you'd got fish in the pool, Kat!"

"The little monsters made some out of foam sponge yesterday and put them in for a swim," chuckled Katie. "They must look lifelike if they've fooled the heron."

"He's flying off now," said Sara. "He must have realized they aren't real."

"Look at Timmy, I mean Tammy," said Katie. "She's right up against the cage door watching the heron. I bet she's wondering what it is!"

"She's squeaking," said Sara, as they reached the cage.

"Mm," smiled Katie. "Just have a quick peep, Scarer, then we'll leave them alone. I think Tammy's telling her babies she doesn't know what the big flying shape is, but there's no need for them to be frightened of it."

But of course, Tammy *did* know what it was! She knew all about the grey feathers on tall sticks, and she was promising her babies she'd tell *them* a story about him when they were a little bit older.

"And about Mr and Mrs Kingfisher and their smelly nesting hole … and Frog … and Water Vole," she squeaked. "It was quite an adventure, the day I met them all. Quite a frightening adventure at times…" Tammy shuddered. "I think the very worst bit was when I thought I was lost…"

The babies looked solemnly at their mother. Tammy stopped shuddering and said, "I was lucky. Katie found me and brought me safely home. But," she added,

nuzzling each baby in turn, "when you grow up, you must promise *never* to wander away from your home like I did. Home is the best place in the world."

And Tammy snuffled happily as she gazed round her cage, at the branches to gnaw at, the log to scramble over, her food dishes, her water bottle, the cosy sleeping area…

Tammy blinked, then she yawned. And, before long, she was asleep with her three pretty babies snuggling contentedly against her.

The End